MR DOG

AND THE KITTEN CATASTROPHE

First published in Great Britain by
HarperCollins *Children's Books* in 2021
HarperCollins *Children's Books* is a division of HarperCollins*Publishers* Ltd
1 London Bridge Street
London SE1 9GF

www.harpercollins.co.uk

HarperCollins*Publishers*
1st Floor, Watermarque Building, Ringsend Road
Dublin 4, Ireland

1

ISBN 978–0–00–840829–9

A CIP catalogue record for this title is available from the British Library.

Printed and bound in England by CPI Group (UK) Ltd, Croydon, CR0 4YY

MIX
Paper from
responsible sources
FSC™ C007454

This book is produced from independently certified FSC™ paper
to ensure responsible forest management.

For more information visit: www.harpercollins.co.uk/green

MR DOG
AND THE KITTEN CATASTROPHE

BEN FOGLE

with Steve Cole

Illustrated by Nikolas Ilic

HarperCollins *Children's Books*

About the Author

BEN FOGLE is a broadcaster and seasoned adventurer. A modern-day nomad and journeyman, he has travelled to more than a hundred countries and accomplished amazing feats; from swimming with crocodiles to rowing three thousand miles across the Atlantic Ocean; from crossing Antarctica on foot to surviving a year as a castaway on a remote Hebridean island. Most recently, Ben climbed Mount Everest. Oh, and he LOVES dogs.

Books by Ben Fogle

MR DOG AND THE RABBIT HABIT

MR DOG AND THE SEAL DEAL

MR DOG AND A HEDGE CALLED HOG

MR DOG AND THE FARAWAY FOX

MR DOG AND A DEER FRIEND

For Inca, Maggi and Bica

Chapter One

THE FOREST MONSTER

'Help!' came a squeak from the gloom of the forest. 'There's a monster coming!'

Mr Dog's shaggy ears shot up in the air. He had come to this Welsh forest for some peace, quiet and berries (not necessarily in that order). He hadn't expected to find a monster on the loose!

'Help!' came another squeak, closer now. 'It's catching up!'

Mr Dog was up and alert in a moment. He was a scruffy mutt, black all over save for his white muzzle and two front paws. 'Who's there?' he woofed. 'I'm Mr Dog. I'll help if I can!'

The next moment, two tiny fieldmice came running into the forest clearing. 'Help us, Mr Dog! Help us!' they squealed.

Mr Dog looked down at the trembling creatures. They had brown-flecked fur and white tummies, with large ears and twitching whiskers.

Their eyes were big and bright and berry-black.

'Don't be afraid,' said Mr Dog. 'What's all this about a monster?'

'It chased us through the woods!' piped up one of the mice.

'It's furry and frightening!' said the second. 'We must hide!'

Before Mr Dog could woof another word, both mice had rushed beneath his black brushy tail. 'You poor mice really are scared, aren't you?' murmured Mr Dog. He gulped as the sound of snapping twigs and rustling bushes grew closer. 'But I'm a friend to all animals. And I'm sure monsters are a kind of animal too!'

Mr Dog puffed up his chest and lowered

his bushy brows in the hope it made him look

scarier. But his eyes widened in surprise as a

stocky, stripy beast burst into the forest clearing.

It stopped at the sight of Mr Dog and stared at

him with amber eyes.

At first glance, this 'monster' looked like a

tabby kitten the size of a house cat. But its eyes

were far fiercer. Its body was solid and sturdy

with thick wavy stripes and powerful jaws. Its tail

was thicker than a normal cat's and had a blunt

black tip.

'Where are those two mice?' said the cat-monster.

That's funny, thought Mr Dog. *He sounds Scottish but we're in the middle of Wales.*

'Two mice?' Mr Dog could feel the little rodents shivering under his tail, but kept smiling. 'Sorry, old chap. Never heard of them. I'm Mr Dog. Who are you?'

'I'm Angus,' said the oversized kitten. 'I'm a Scottish wildcat, you know.'

'I did *not* know.' Mr Dog beamed. 'I've been to Scotland. I hear its wildcats are extremely rare. I certainly didn't expect to meet one in a wet wood in Wales!' With a quick wag of his

tail, he swept some old leaves over the mice
to keep them hidden, then padded over to
Angus.

Angus hissed at him, revealing sharp, pointed
fangs. 'Keep back, doggy! Or I'll . . .' He trailed
off, suddenly distracted. 'Oh, hey! It's a flappy
thing.' The wildcat watched, fascinated, as a wood
warbler flitted between some branches high
above. 'Oooh, look! That flappy thing is so fast!'

Mr Dog smiled. Angus was big, but his
attention span was short – he was still very much
a kitten at heart!

'If you think that bird has got some moves,
Angus – watch this!' said Mr Dog. He began to

1

dance a little jig on his hind paws. Angus watched

as if hypnotised, a smile on his face. And while

the 'monster' was distracted, the little fieldmice

crept from the clearing and vanished into the

thicker forest.

Once Mr Dog was sure the mice were safe, he stopped dancing. 'Now then, Angus,' he said, 'can you tell me what a rare Scottish wildcat kitten is doing in the Brecon Beacons?'

'I was captured,' said Angus crossly. 'Weeks ago, this lady called Noel lured me into a cage. She took me to live with other locked-up animals in a big house.'

Mr Dog frowned. 'What sort of animals?'

'All sorts,' said Angus. A beetle crawled past his paws. 'Oooh! Look. A little wiggly thing!'

'Never mind that beetle!' said Mr Dog. 'If you were locked up by this Noel lady, how did you get out?'

9

'A few days ago, there was a terrible storm,' said Angus.

'I remember,' said Mr Dog. 'I had to shelter in a log pile with a squirrel. Almost drove me nuts!' He chuckled at his little joke. Angus stared blankly. 'I'm sorry. Do go on.'

'Well, the storm blew down a tree and it hit the fence in our exercise yard.' The kitten's eyes were bright with excitement. 'Some of the animals escaped – including my mama! I ran after her . . . but I couldn't keep up.'

'What? Your mama left you behind?' Mr Dog was feeling sadder and sadder at Angus's story. 'I'm sure she's been trying to find you.'

'Noel's trying to find me too,' said Angus. 'She has people helping her. They feed us. Exercise us. Clean us out.' The kitten sighed. 'Then they lock us up again.'

'It sounds like you've escaped from a prison!' Mr Dog declared. 'I don't like the sound of Noel and her helpers one bit . . .' Suddenly, his ears pricked at the sound of movement nearby. 'Wait. I hear something.'

Angus sniffed the air. 'Aye. You're right. Humans.'

Mr Dog nodded. 'Is it Nasty Noel and the rest?'

'I'm not sure,' Angus admitted. 'I don't recognise their smell.'

'You wait here, out of sight,' said Mr Dog. 'I'll investigate.'

'Thanks, Mr Dog!' Angus jumped up on to a tree branch and hid in the leaves. 'You're so brave!'

'Some say the D-O-G in my name stands for Daring Old Gent,' said Mr Dog with a grin. He crept off through the undergrowth.

Soon he could hear human voices. They belonged to a man and a woman.

'We have to find those wild animals,' said the man.

'And we have to find them fast,' a woman agreed. 'Don't forget – start shooting the second you see them . . .'

'Shooting?' Mr Dog couldn't believe his ears. 'It sounds like Angus and his mama are in even greater danger than I thought. But I'll help them and any other animal in danger – or my name's not Mr Dog!'

Chapter Two

FINDING MAMA

Mr Dog crawled away from the mysterious couple and back to the clearing where he'd left Angus. The wildcat kitten had come out of hiding. He was rolling around in the leaves.

'Angus!' hissed Mr Dog. 'I told you to stay out of sight!'

'Oooh, look. A stick!' The kitten grabbed it with his front paws and rolled on to his back, gnawing on it. 'Mmmm. Sticky.'

Mr Dog sighed. 'We need to go, Angus. I heard a man and a woman say they'll shoot any wild animals they find.'

Angus looked at him innocently. 'What does "shoot" mean?'

'Nothing good,' said Mr Dog with a shudder. 'Now, we must find your mama as quickly as possible. Let's follow our noses and see where they lead.'

Together they moved cautiously through the

forest. It was mid-morning and the early autumn

sunlight was dappled under the thick, leafy

branches. Mr Dog's nose twitched with all sorts

of strange scents. Unusual animals had passed

this way, but not recently.

'I can't hear anyone moving about in this part

of the forest,' said Angus.

Mr Dog raised his eyebrows. 'Could you really hear them if they were?'

'Sure! We Scottish wildcats have super-senses,' Angus said proudly. 'I heard Noel tell someone on the telephone.'

'Oh yes?' said Mr Dog. 'What else did she say?'

'She said I was worth thousands and that she'd sell me to the buyest hidder.'

'The buyest hidder?' Mr Dog gasped. 'You mean the *highest bidder*!'

'That's what I said,' Angus protested.

Mr Dog was starting to understand. He had heard about people who captured wild animals to sell as exotic pets. The more unusual the animal, the more desirable it was for certain

collectors to own – and the more money

it was worth to the likes of Nasty Noel. Mr

Dog's ears drooped. *Those poor wild animals!*

he thought. Such creatures weren't meant

to be cooped up and cared for by humans,

however well meaning. They should be roaming

freely in their native habitats among their own

kind.

'Well, first things first, Angus,' said Mr Dog.

'You'll feel much better when you're back with

your mother . . .'

'Wait!' Angus said suddenly. He was holding

very still with his body low to the ground. 'I can

feel vibrations. The sort my mama makes when she prowls about.'

'Bless my nose!' said Mr Dog. 'What sensitive paws you must have.'

'Mama's close!' Angus started chasing his tail in a circle. 'She's close, she's close!'

Suddenly, he threw back his head and gave a loud, rasping miaow.

'MIAOWWWWwwww!'

'Angus, don't call out to her!' Mr Dog flattened his ears to his head. 'Hunters might hear you.'

'Mama could eat them for breakfast!' Angus retorted. 'I can smell her . . . this way!'

Mr Dog followed him, sniffing the air too. Soon his nose was tingling with a strong, musky smell unlike any he had smelled before. *It's very different from Angus's scent,* he thought.

But then he heard the crunch and crackle of branches close by.

'Come on!' Mr Dog used his nose to scoop up Angus and toss him on to his back. 'Humans again and they're coming this way!' He quickly carried the kitten behind a large oak and burrowed under the ivy that covered its base.

Mr Dog and Angus were hidden from sight with seconds to spare. They held their breath as a short, stocky man stepped out of the undergrowth. Another man, taller and younger, followed. Both were carrying strange handguns and had rifles strapped to their backs.

'We're getting closer, Desi,' said the stocky man. 'I can sense it.'

'We'd better be, Sawyer,' Desi replied. 'If we don't bring back those animals, Noel will put *us* in the cages!'

'Desi and Sawyer,' Angus whispered. 'Are they the people you saw before?'

'No,' hissed Mr Dog. 'Which means there are

at least four hunters looking for you and your friends.'

'Four?' Angus tried counting that far on his paws, but lost track and gave up. 'I'm sorry, Mr Dog. I should've picked up their scent. My nostrils must have been too full of mama-cat smell!'

'I didn't smell them either,' Mr Dog assured him. 'Hunters often use a dirt wash to hide their scent from animals . . .'

Suddenly, there was a crackle of static. Sawyer, the stocky man, pulled a walkie-talkie from his back pocket. A woman's voice squawked out: 'This is Noel for Sawyer. Sawyer, come in.'

'Go ahead, Noel,' said Sawyer into the radio.

'Have you caught the runaways?' Noel demanded. 'Over.'

Sawyer swapped an awkward look with Desi. 'On it, Noel. Currently searching the western quarter of the property. Over.'

Noel did not sound happy. 'I'm calling in help so we have a bigger search party,' she said. 'Keep me updated. Noel out.'

The radio went silent and Sawyer shoved it back in his pocket.

'Dear me,' whispered Mr Dog. '*More* hunters on the way!'

Desi was crouching down beside a patch of

mud. 'There's a paw print here, Sawyer.'

Sawyer came over to see. 'That's just a dog. Come on. Looks like the undergrowth's been broken over there . . .'

The two men set off stealthily. Mr Dog and Angus watched them go from their hiding place.

'*Just* a dog. How dare he!' Mr Dog grumbled. 'Come on. With extra hunters on the way, we must stay alert . . .' His nose twitched. The strange, exotic smell was much stronger now.

'Mama!' cried Angus.

Mr Dog yelped in alarm as a large, lean and

lanky creature crashed into the clearing. She

had yellow fur, covered in black spots, and long

legs. Her tail was narrow, her ears were short and

round and her amber eyes narrowed as she gave a

throaty roar.

'That's not your mama, Angus!' Mr Dog

whispered, not daring to move. 'It's . . .

it's a *cheetah*!'

Chapter Three

SPOTTED DANGER

The cheetah's eyes were fixed on Mr Dog. Her teeth were bared. A low growl was building in her throat.

Mr Dog stayed very still. He knew that cheetahs could reach speeds of up to seventy miles an hour. *This big cat should be chasing down*

gazelles in the African savannah, he thought, *not little woofers in a wood!*

'There you are, Mama!' Angus pranced up to the cheetah and nuzzled his head against her side. She looked down and licked him.

Mr Dog stared in surprise. He guessed that when Angus had been taken from his real mama, he'd looked to the nearest big cat for a replacement. Perhaps the cheetah had lost her own cubs and Angus reminded her of them? Mr Dog felt sad and angry that both these magnificent cats had been taken from their homes to be sold on as pets!

The cheetah took a step closer to Mr Dog and he gulped. 'Er, Angus?' he said quietly. 'Could you ask your mama not to eat me, please? I really wouldn't taste good. I'm fairly sure that the D-O-G part of my name stands for "Disgusting Old Gristle"!'

The warning was in vain. The cheetah lunged at him! Mr Dog jumped aside just in time. He guessed the cheetah had only missed him because she was cold, confused and weak with hunger. Not wanting to give her time to try again, Mr Dog scrambled up into a tree and hid on a leafy branch.

'Mama, don't eat him!' Angus jumped on to the cheetah's back. 'Mr Dog is a friend. He can't help us if he's inside your tummy!'

The cheetah looked up at Mr Dog. 'You really want to help us?' she growled. 'Why?'

'Because I don't believe that wild animals should be kept as pets,' said Mr Dog. 'Did Nasty

Noel catch you like she caught Angus?'

The cheetah shook her head. 'I was caught by poachers and they *sold* me to Noel. She knows someone who wants to buy a big cat. He'll give her more money than she paid for me.'

'Only if you're caught again,' said Mr Dog.

But, even as he spoke, he caught movement from across the clearing. The two hunters – Desi and Sawyer – must have heard the growling.

They had come back!

The cheetah roared and moved in front of Angus. She made ready to charge at the hunters . . .

THUPP! Desi fired one of his guns. It shot a

dart with a pink feathered tip into the cheetah's chest. She staggered back and flopped down on her side.

'Got her!' cried Sawyer.

Those guns fire tranquilliser darts! Mr Dog realised. *Darts that make the cheetah sleepy and easy to catch.*

'Mama!' Angus wailed. He ran to her and nuzzled his head against her belly.

'Now for the wildcat.' Desi aimed his tranquilliser gun at Angus. 'Just hold still, little guy . . .'

But, before Desi could shoot, Mr Dog burst out of his leafy hiding place, barking wildly!

The angry mutt flew through the air and struck Desi's chest with his two front paws, knocking him over backwards.

'It's time to use my head!' Mr Dog declared. He bounced back up and head-butted Sawyer in the stomach. The man gasped in surprise and

staggered back into a tree,

dropping the gun.

'Angus, come on!' woofed Mr Dog. 'We can't

help your mama now.'

'What?' asked the upset kitten.

'RUN!' Mr Dog barked so loudly that Angus

nearly turned a somersault. But it gave him the shock he needed to burst into action – just as Desi scrambled to his feet and raised his tranquilliser gun.

'Duck!' yapped Mr Dog.

'Ooh, a duck?' Angus stopped running and looked around. 'Where?'

Mr Dog whopped the wildcat kitten with his tail and knocked him aside – and just in time! *THUPP!* Another dart came whizzing past and struck a tree, just centimetres from Angus. The kitten jumped up and raced away into the undergrowth. Breathlessly, Mr Dog followed him.

Angus moved like furry lightning! Mr Dog had to run full pelt to keep up – but he wasn't as good at climbing trees as the wildcat kitten, or at pushing through thorny brambles. He soon lost sight of him and didn't dare bark in case more hunters were close by.

It was a good call because Mr Dog soon heard voices. It was the man and the woman he'd spotted earlier! They were about again!

'I wish we were better trackers,' said the woman.

The man sighed in agreement. 'We've found nothing worth shooting all day . . .'

'Nothing worth shooting?' muttered Mr Dog.

'How can they be so horrid? I've *got* to find Angus and the other wild animals before they're captured, hurt . . . or worse!'

Chapter Four

A STRANGE DISCOVERY

Mr Dog held still, waiting for the couple to move away. He was longing to find Angus, but didn't want to take the chance of leading the hunters to him.

The couple didn't move for some time, talking about the best light to shoot in, and how they hoped they could get clear shots.

'Beastly humans,' muttered Mr Dog.

But then the woman said something strange. 'The public need to know what Noel's up to. If we get proper evidence, the police will have to do something.'

'The proper evidence is inside her house,' said the man. 'But Noel's got so much security – it's like she lives inside an army camp.'

'The animals got out,' said the woman. 'It stands to reason we can get in somehow . . .'

She stopped talking as a distant roar carried across the woods. *Another wild animal*, thought Mr Dog.

'Come on,' the woman told her companion. 'If we can find whatever that is before Noel's hunters do, we might get something worth shooting after all . . .'

The couple stomped away noisily through the woodland.

Mr Dog stepped out of hiding, deep in thought. 'It sounds as if these people are working *against* Nasty Noel,' he said to himself. 'But they're still talking about shooting things. Perhaps they're her rivals? Maybe they want to catch and sell the wild animals themselves!'

Wishing he knew more about what was

going on, Mr Dog set off again in search
of Angus. Soon his keen nose twitched at
a strong smell coming from a tree at
kitten height. Angus must have rubbed
his cheek glands against the bark as all
wildcats did, leaving his scent as a trail
to follow! Sniffing away, Mr Dog followed
his nose. When the smell grew fainter,
he noticed scratches in the tree trunks –
more territorial markings left behind
by a growing wildcat.

Mr Dog became completely engrossed
in following Angus's trail. Finally he heard a
mournful little cry up ahead. 'Hello . . . ?'

'Angus!' Mr Dog woofed happily and bounded

over to the wildcat kitten. 'There you are!'

'And there YOU are!' Angus licked his ear with

his rough, scratchy tongue. 'But how are we going

to help Mama, Mr Dog?'

'That's a good question,' said Mr Dog sadly. 'I suppose she's been taken back to Noel's house. She'll be locked up in her cage again by now.' He looked at Angus. 'Do you know your way there?'

At once, the kitten grew afraid. 'I don't want to go back, Mr Dog!'

'You won't have to,' Mr Dog assured him. 'I just want to have a sniff about. I overheard that strange shooting couple talking about how much security Noel has. But what's designed to keep out humans may not keep out a dashing dog like me!'

'Why would you want to get inside Noel's

house?' asked Angus.

Mr Dog gave a sly smile. 'Because there's evidence inside the house that would prove to the police that she's dealing illegally in wild animals. If I can just find it and get it to the police somehow . . .' Mr Dog sighed. His plan sounded far-fetched even to his own floppy ears! But he couldn't think of any other way to help.

I have *to try!* he thought.

Angus was sniffing the air. 'I think Noel's house is this way,' he said, and set off through the undergrowth – slowly and carefully this time.

Thirty minutes later, they came to a narrow track that wound through the forest. The dried mud was marked with tyre tracks.

'Aha!' said Mr Dog. 'This must be the way to Noel's countryside camp.'

Together the two animals trotted along the path. Soon they heard a loud, familiar roar from up ahead, out of sight beyond a bend in the track.

'Mama!' Angus beamed and rasped a miaow

back as loudly as he could. 'Did you hear that, Mr

Dog? Mama's all right, and she's close by!'

RAWRRR! came the growl of the cheetah.

Angus quickly rushed off in the

direction of the sound.

RAWRRR!

'Wait,' woofed Mr Dog. 'Remember, Angus,

you must be careful!'

Mr Dog sped after the impetuous kitten. As he

rounded the corner, he frowned. A pick-up truck

was parked in the middle of the mud track. The

passenger and driver's doors were wide open.

No one seemed to be inside, but the cheetah was locked up in a steel cage in the back. She lay on her side with her eyes closed, breathing softly.

'Look, Mr Dog!' Angus was dancing with excitement round the back of the pick-up. 'It's Mama!'

'But why has she been left here alone on the track?' Mr Dog wondered as he padded closer. 'Perhaps the truck broke down, and the driver's gone to get help . . . ?'

RAWRRR! The growl sounded again.

'Wow,' said Angus. 'Mama can roar in her sleep without moving her mouth!'

Mr Dog frowned. He realised that the growls had come from *inside* the pick-up. They were playing through the truck's speakers.

'Angus, run!' barked Mr Dog. 'Something's wrong!'

'No good woofing now, you mangy mutt!' Desi the hunter burst out from behind the cheetah cage on the pick-up and hurled a net over Angus. 'Ha! The trap worked!'

Angus struggled angrily in the net, but only got more tangled up. 'Mr Dog!' he mewed. 'Help me!'

Teeth bared and growling, Mr Dog was already running forward.

But then another net was thrown over *him*. It stopped him in his tracks. He rolled over and saw the other hunter, Sawyer, smiling down. 'That's fixed you, doggy!'

Mr Dog barked ferociously as he strained to get free, but the net was too strong.

Just like Angus, he was caught in the hunters' trap!

Chapter Five

THE MIGHTY ZEUS!

Mr Dog gnawed at the net, but he knew the links were too tough for his teeth to break through. He watched helplessly as Desi put on long leather gloves and picked up Angus. The little wildcat struggled and scratched, but the leather protected Desi's hands. Sawyer crossed to the pick-up and pulled out a carry-case. Desi bundled Angus inside and then Sawyer slammed the door shut.

'There!' said Desi. 'That should hold him. The kitten couldn't resist the sound of his adopted mum, just as you said, Sawyer.'

'Let's spread the good news.' Sawyer pulled out his radio. 'Noel? Come in, Noel.'

'Go for Noel,' came the woman's familiar voice. 'This had better be good news.'

'The best,' said Sawyer. 'Cheetah and wildcat safely acquired. Over.'

'About time,' said Noel. 'My buyer for the wildcat wants to collect him this evening . . .'

A buyer for Angus? Mr Dog's ears almost jumped off his head. 'Oh, no!'

'Bring the cats here straight away,' Noel ordered. 'Then get back out and find Zeus.'

'Copy that. Bringing in the cats. Out.' Sawyer tucked the radio back in his pocket. 'Never grateful, is she?'

'Who cares, as long as she keeps paying us,' said Desi.

Angus's little face was pressed up against the side of the cage.

'Mr Dog! Did you hear Noel? She's going to sell me. Tonight!'

'Don't worry, Angus!' barked Mr Dog. 'I'll get you out of there somehow!'

The hunters looked up at the sound of the mewing and barking. Desi nodded at Mr Dog. 'What shall we do with the pooch?'

'Leave him where he is,' said Sawyer, getting into the driver's seat. 'We'll pick him up later. We might need some live bait to bring Zeus out of hiding . . .'

Mr Dog gulped hard. 'I don't like the sound of that,' he whimpered. 'Just who or what *is* Zeus?'

Desi laughed and got inside the pick-up. As the door closed, Mr Dog couldn't hear the rest of the hunters' conversation. He watched miserably as the truck trundled away up the track and was soon lost from sight.

Mr Dog clawed at the ground beneath him. If he couldn't break through the net, perhaps he could burrow under it? He set to work with his paws.

It was no good. The ground was too hard and rocky. Nevertheless, Mr Dog kept trying. 'I can't give up,' he panted. 'Angus is depending on me . . . and all the other animals need my help too!'

But suddenly he heard a long, deep growl. It set the hairs on his back standing on end.

Thump! Thump! Crash! Heavy, lumbering footsteps were coming towards him. Foliage was being forced out of the way.

Mr Dog gulped. 'All the other animals need my help . . . but I could certainly use some myself with whatever it is that's coming!' He flattened his ears and dug harder.

Seconds later, with the loudest growl yet, an enormous, terrifying animal burst out of the bracken.

It was a brown and shaggy grizzly bear!

The bear stood fully eight feet tall. A powerful hump rounded out his shoulders. His paws were edged with long, curved claws. He fixed his dark eyes on Mr Dog, still caught in the net. The bear's jaws opened wide as he lumbered closer.

This brute will munch me up in a moment! thought Mr Dog as the giant loomed over him. 'Forgive me, Angus,' he said, closing his eyes. 'It looks like my adventures are over . . .'

'Hello, dog,' said the bear politely. 'What are you doing in that funny bag?'

Mr Dog felt a surge of hope. This giant bear actually sounded quite friendly! 'Er . . . it's not a bag. It's a net. A hunter threw it over me, and now I'm stuck.'

The bear seemed to think about this. 'Would you like me to take the net off you?'

Mr Dog gave his biggest, doggiest grin. 'Oh, yes, please.'

With a grunt, the grizzly pulled off the metal net and tossed it into a bush at the side of the track.

'Thank you!' Mr Dog jumped up. 'My name's Mr Dog. The D-O-G part is currently short for

Dramatically, Overwhelmingly Grateful!' He sat on his haunches and bowed his head. 'Who are you?'

'Zeus,' said the bear. 'The Mighty Zeus, to be precise. That's what Noel calls me.' He paused. 'Do you have a tuna sandwich?'

'Er, not on me,' Mr Dog confessed.

'That's a shame,' said Zeus. 'I like sandwiches.'

'I'm surprised,' said Mr Dog. 'I thought a big wild bear like you would be a fierce hunter.'

'Eating something raw? Ugh! No, thank you.' Zeus shook his huge head. 'You see, I'm a dancing bear.' He did a little jig as if to prove it, then dropped down on to all fours beside Mr

Dog. 'I dance for my supper. I don't hunt for it.'

'When were you taken from the wild?' asked Mr Dog.

'As a cub,' Zeus replied. 'I used to belong to a little zoo, but they couldn't afford to keep me. They sold me to Noel a couple of years ago. She's been training me. Now she plans to sell me to a wealthy customer whose daughters want a dancing bear.' He sighed. 'That's why I ran away the first chance I got. But I haven't found a single tuna sandwich out here in the wild, and I'm getting very hungry . . .'

Mr Dog felt sad and angry that such a magnificent animal had never been allowed to roam wild in his native habitat – to hunt and feed as other bears did. His dancing was very good, of course – but bears weren't put on the planet to make humans laugh and point.

'Nasty Noel has a lot to answer for,' Mr Dog said sadly. 'I'm afraid her hunters have just recaptured my friend Angus.'

'That sparky kitten?' Zeus sighed. 'Oh, dear.'

'Look!' came a woman's whisper from behind them. 'We've found the bear!'

With a jump, Mr Dog turned to find the mysterious couple he'd run into twice before, watching from the cover of the forest.

'Finally,' said the man, pulling something

dark and heavy from his bag. 'Something worth shooting!'

Mr Dog yelped. 'Run for it, Zeus! Or those two will get us for sure!'

Chapter Six

THE SANDWICH STRUGGLE

Mr Dog dived for the trees at the side of the track. But Zeus didn't follow. He reared up on his back legs as the man and the woman came out from the forest.

'What are you doing, Zeus?' Mr Dog barked urgently. 'Run!'

'It's all right,' said Zeus calmly. 'They're not shooting bullets. They're only shooting video!'

'What?' Mr Dog looked at the couple. Sure enough, he saw that they weren't pointing guns at all. They were carrying fancy TV cameras!

'I can smell sandwiches in their backpacks,' said Zeus. He started to dance, lumbering first one way, and then the other. 'Perhaps I can earn one with my act!'

'We got lucky at last!' said the woman. 'I've heard that the bear is the biggest of Noel's illegal animal collection. Shoot all the footage you can, Mike.'

'I will!' Mike grinned. 'This bear certainly isn't shy, is he? This will look great in our TV documentary, Iona!'

Mr Dog could hardly believe his eyes, seeing the bear perform that way for the camera. But his ears pricked when he heard the mention of a TV documentary. Suddenly, things made more sense. Mike and Iona must be making a film about Nasty Noel's naughty animal activities. They were looking for evidence of what she'd been getting up to.

But that evidence could only be inside Noel's house. Without it, all they really had was film of a bear dancing in Welsh woodland. That wouldn't help Angus, his mama and all the other exotic animals Noel had under lock and key!

Zeus,' said Mr Dog, 'I have to get into Noel's house and try to help the other animals. Perhaps

I can sneak in if you create a distraction?'

The big, burly bear stopped dancing for a moment and thought. 'I need a sandwich first,' he said.

'Then I shall help you get it!' said Mr Dog. He trotted up to Iona and Mike with his most appealing, big-eyed doggy face. He began to join Zeus in a little dance on his back legs. Then he padded closer and held up a paw.

'I thought I saw this dog earlier,' said Mike, lowering his camera as he chuckled. 'He's quite a performer too.'

'No collar, just a hanky round his neck,' noted Iona. She crouched beside Mr Dog. 'Perhaps he's a stray. Or . . . perhaps he belongs to Noel?'

Mr Dog yipped crossly. *How dare you!* he said, but of course it only came out as an indignant whine.

'If he *is* Noel's dog, perhaps he ran away in the storm like the other animals,' said Mike. 'If we catch him and return him, Noel might actually let us into her home.'

'More likely she'd take one look at our cameras and chuck us off her land,' said Iona. Then she smiled and started rummaging about in her backpack. 'Although maybe bringing the dog to her is still a good idea . . .'

No, it's a very bad *idea,* Mr Dog longed to tell her. *Because I am NOT Noel's dog! And I hate to think what she'll do to me if you hand me over!* Deciding it was time to go, he quickly pushed his nose into the rucksack and sniffed out a brown bag with sandwiches inside.

'Forgive me,' said Mr Dog, 'but I believe this bear's need is greater than yours!' He grabbed the bag in his jaws and pulled it out.

'Hey, cheeky!' Iona had taken something from the backpack herself, but Mr Dog couldn't see what it was. She grabbed hold of Mr Dog's makeshift collar and fiddled with it. 'I have something to give you, but it's not something you can eat . . .'

'Unhand me, madam!' Mr Dog pulled quickly away from her and ran off back to the bear with his purloined prize. 'Come on, Zeus. I have the sandwiches. Let's go!'

'Wait!' called Iona. 'Don't just run off!' She made to go after him, but Zeus suddenly roared at Iona which stopped her in her tracks.

Then he turned, dropped to all fours, and crashed through the undergrowth with Mr Dog.

Iona groaned. 'They're getting away, Mike!'

'Thanks for the sandwich,' Mr Dog yapped back, but of course to human ears it came out only as, '*Wuff-wuff WUFF!*'

The massive bear cleared a path through the overgrown parts of the wood that made it easy for Mr Dog to follow. When they were a good distance away from Mike and Iona, the two animals stopped. Mr Dog offered Zeus the sandwiches and the bear accepted them eagerly.

'Hmmm,' said Zeus as he chewed and gulped down his food. 'Needs more mayo.'

'What *we* need is time,' said Mr Dog. It was starting to get dark. 'Angus's buyer might already have arrived.'

'Well, we're not far from Noel's house now,' said Zeus. 'The outer wall is just the other side of those trees. There's a door leading to the exercise yard.'

'Hurrah!' Mr Dog grinned. 'Now you've finished your dinner – let's take a look.'

He poked his nose out from the treeline. Ahead of him, in the late evening gloom, he could make out a large, imposing wall. He edged out further.

Suddenly, a dazzling light snapped on – like a giant's spotlight – and was trained right at him.

'Intruder detected!' came a deep, gruff shout.

Mr Dog dropped to the ground. 'Oh, no!' he wuffed. 'I've been caught already!'

Chapter Seven

OUT OF THE WOODS

Blinded by the powerful light, Mr Dog heard movement behind him. Was it a hunter closing in?

No. It was Zeus!

'Well done, humans!' the bear growled. 'You've detected an intruder. Now, come and get me!'

'It's the bear!' someone yelled. 'After him!'

But Zeus had already turned and gone crashing back through the trees.

A female hunter spoke into a radio: 'Come in, Noel. This is Patrol Three outside exercise yard. Bear sighted breaking cover.'

'Leave Desi on guard at the door. The rest of you – get after Zeus!' Nasty Noel's voice squawked out. 'My buyer is arriving any time now. I want my property secure and that bear safely out of the way!'

'In pursuit,' the woman said gruffly. 'Over.'

Mr Dog quickly crawled forward until he bumped up against the wall. As he did so, he heard heavy boots clumping across the grass, heading towards the trees, and after Zeus.

The grizzly had provided the perfect distraction, and Mr Dog knew he couldn't waste it.

The security light was shut off and darkness returned. Mr Dog blinked to clear his vision and thought hard. Earlier, in the clearing, he'd heard Noel say that she was calling for backup. It sounded as if she must have at least three groups of hunters posted outside her home, keeping exits and entrances secure for her visitors – or rather her customers.

Mr Dog sneaked a look along the wall. Sure enough, Desi stood outside the solid oak door that must lead to the exercise yard. The hunter was carrying a tranquilliser gun. It would be almost impossible for even the cleverest dog to sneak in now . . .

Then he heard a small commotion on the other side of the wall. The scuffle was followed by a frantic female voice. 'No! Get back here, you horrid little furball!' The woman was answered by a fierce and familiar feline yowl . . .

Mr Dog grinned. 'Angus!'

There was a sudden banging on the inside of the door. 'Desi? It's me, Jan, the groomer. That little wildcat has got loose. Help me catch it!'

Desi groaned. 'Seriously?'

'I was making him look his best for his buyer when he jumped out of his carry-case!' Jan said. 'The buyer's paying thousands of pounds for the little devil, so Noel wants him looking his best.'

'Who'd pay so much for an oversized pussycat?' Desi grumbled.

'Someone with more money than sense. They just want to show off that they own a special animal as a pet,' said Jan. 'And since they pay Noel, and Noel pays our wages, you'd better help me find him!'

'All right.' Desi put his gun in its holster, pulled out a key ring jangling with keys and started to unlock the door to the exercise yard.

Mr Dog watched closely. 'I think my chances

of getting inside just went up a little!'

He crept closer . . .

Desi turned the key and then pulled it out of the lock as he twisted the door handle. Mr Dog raced up and barked at top volume! Desi got such a shock he dropped the keys. Mr Dog's jaws clamped down on the metal ring before it could hit the ground.

'Not you again!' Desi shouted. He reached for the gun in his holster. But Mr Dog jumped up and pushed the man back against the door. It crashed open under his weight and he fell through into the exercise yard. Desi knocked into Jan the groomer, who landed hard on her bottom with a cry.

'Angus?' With the key ring clamped in his teeth, Mr Dog stared all round the exercise yard. 'Angus, where are you?'

'Mr Dog? I'm here!' The big amber eyes of a Scottish wildcat kitten peered out from behind a low stone bath where animals were washed. 'I'm so glad to see you!'

'I'm glad to see you too,' Mr Dog told him, rushing over. 'I can't believe you're free!'

'Only just.' Angus hopped out of hiding. A thick collar had been placed round the kitten's neck, and a long chain lead dragged along the ground behind him. 'The groomer hauled me out here to give me a bath – but I got away. Baths, huh! I'm a wildcat, not a neat little kitty.'

But Mr Dog hardly heard. He was trying to plan their next move. He had come here for evidence of Nasty Noel's wild pet trade that he could take back to Mike and Iona – he hadn't expected that Angus would get free! Now, with the buyer on the way, Mr Dog knew he couldn't risk the wildcat being captured again. He had to help Angus reach the safety of the woods.

But Desi and Jan were already climbing to their feet.

'Come on,' said Mr Dog. 'Let's get out of here!'

'Another daring escape!' Angus's eyes were bright with excitement. 'Let's go – urk!'

His lead had caught on one of the ornamental designs on the side of the stone bath. Angus gasped and went cross-eyed as he kept trying to pull free.

'Wait! Let me help . . .' Still holding the keys in his mouth, Mr Dog nudged the lead with his nose and freed the little wildcat.

But a loud *SLAM* told Mr Dog it was too late to get away. Jan had run over and closed the door. Desi was pulling out his gun.

'Wait,' Jan snapped. 'We can't risk injuring the cat before a sale. But that crazy stray dog is a different matter. Get it!'

Chapter Eight

KITTEN CATASTROPHE!

Mr Dog leaped behind the stone bath as Desi fired a tranquilliser dart. Angus joined him a second later. *BAM!* The dart bounced off the ornate stonework.

'Well, we can't get back to the woods now,' said Mr Dog, 'so we'll just have to get inside the house instead.' He put a paw on the collar and chain around Angus's neck. 'Can you *lead* the way?'

'It's through that door over there,' said Angus. 'Ready?'

Desi was advancing. Mr Dog and Angus burst into a four-legged sprint and shot across the courtyard. Mr Dog tried to zigzag as he ran so he was harder to hit. Another dart went whizzing overhead and bounced off a flowerpot. Angus  jumped over the dart and zoomed through the door. Mr Dog followed him in, then reared up and used his front paws to push the door shut behind them. He dropped the key ring on the floor.

They were in a storeroom full of different kinds of animal feed and bedding, from bales of hay to berries and blankets.

'If only I knew which key would lock this door!' said Mr Dog as footsteps sounded on the concrete outside. 'But there's no time. Angus! Help me push over that hay bale!'

Together, with all their strength, they were able to overbalance the bale so it fell against the door and blocked it shut before Desi could open it.

'That was fun!' panted Angus. 'Now what?'

'Without their keys, it should take Jan and Desi longer to get in through another door,' said

Mr Dog. 'Meanwhile, we need somewhere good to hide.'

'Oh! I know, I know! Follow me!' said Angus.

Mr Dog trailed the kitten out of the storeroom and into another room filled with food and water dishes, cages and carry-cases of different sizes, and all sorts of cleaning products. Here was evidence of what a big business Nasty Noel was running.

But it's not like I can just drag all this stuff out and show it to anyone, thought Mr Dog. *So what can I do?*

He followed Angus along a corridor. A strong pong of many different animals filled his nostrils.

The wildcat kitten led him into a large room
with a high glass ceiling. It was like a miniature
zoo! The cheetah lay in a cage next to a pair of
Siberian raccoon dogs, although they looked
more like raccoon *foxes* to Mr Dog's eyes. There

were special snakes and rare lizards in glass

cases . . . a huge empty cage that surely belonged

to Zeus . . . and some marmosets huddled in a

cage that didn't seem big enough for one, let

alone two.

'Poor Mama,' said Angus, rubbing his cheek against the cheetah's cage to leave his scent there. 'I hoped she could tell us a good place to hide. But she's still asleep from that dart.'

'Look at *all* these poor animals!' said Mr Dog sadly. 'None of them should be held in captivity like this.'

'Maybe we could let them out?' said Angus. 'They can live in the countryside here.'

'It's too risky,' said Mr Dog. 'A wildcat is at home in a wood, but many of these animals just don't belong around here . . .'

He was interrupted by the voice of Nasty Noel right beside them: 'Exotic pets! Very rare . . .'

Mr Dog jumped for cover behind a cage. But Angus dived for it at the same time and they bumped their heads together. 'Oof!' they both cried.

Noel went on talking as if she'd not noticed a thing. 'Exotic pets! Very rare. Best price. Keep it secret. Open the cage.' And then she squawked. 'SQUAWK!'

Baffled, Mr Dog looked around – and saw a birdcage dangling from the ceiling. Inside was a beautiful green parrot. She had a rosy orange beak and brilliant blue and red under her wings.

'It *wasn't* Noel talking!' Mr Dog realised. 'It was that parrot! She's an Eclectus parrot unless

I'm very much mistaken . . .' He smiled at Angus. 'And the D-O-G in my name might be short for "Don't Often Get it wrong"!'

'That's Eccles the parrot,' Angus told him. 'She's brilliant at impersonations.'

'And a fast learner,' said Mr Dog. 'She sounded just like Noel.'

'Scottish wildcat, Mr Bernwood,' Eccles went on. 'Scottish wildcat. Very rare.'

'And so are you, Eccles!' said Mr Dog. 'What's more – you are *evidence* that Noel's been selling exotic pets!'

Eccles nodded. 'Very rare,' she said again in Noel's voice. 'Open the cage.'

'I see what you mean, Mr Dog,' said Angus, wiggling his tail in excitement. 'If Eccles could fly to the police and speak in Noel's voice, they'd understand! They'd find out she's been selling pets and come to help us!'

Mr Dog shook his head gently. 'Even if we *could* get Eccles out of her cage . . . even if we could open a window and let her fly outside . . . even if she could find her way to the nearest police station . . . the officers won't do much on the say-so of a parrot!'

'Charming,' huffed Eccles.

'Well, I think it's a *good* idea,' said Angus hotly. 'It's worth a try!'

Before Mr Dog could protest, the plucky kitten had jumped on to a cage. The heavy lead around his neck struck the metal with a loud jangle. Full of determination, Angus sprang towards the heavy curtains and climbed up them. When he was level with the cage, he pounced at it.

But Eccles got a fright when she saw the cat coming for her. She squawked and took off from her perch in a flap of feathers. The cage swung to one side, away from Angus, and he just barely caught hold of it with the tip of his claws, the lead dangling, weighing him down as he swung to and fro.

'Angus!' Mr Dog barked in alarm.

The wildcat kitten did his best to hang on,

scrabbling at the wire bars
of the swinging cage. But
finally he fell off and dropped
down on to a shelf full of
glass specimen jars. **CRASH!**
SMASH! One after another, the jars rolled
off and broke noisily on the floor. The raccoon
dogs yapped and the marmosets shrieked. Eccles
flapped about and squawked like crazy. The noise
and the mess were terrible.

It was a total
kitten catastrophe!

Chapter Nine

NOWHERE TO RUN

Angus sat up on the shelf in a daze. 'Did I do it?' he said hopefully.

'You've gone and done it all right!' groaned Mr Dog as the door swung open. 'Look!'

A very tanned woman in a khaki dress had appeared in the doorway at the far end of the room. Desi the hunter and Jan the groomer were just behind her.

'It's Nasty Noel!' Angus whispered.

'And friends,' Mr Dog agreed.

'Well, well,' Noel snarled. 'I've been trapping and trading wild animals for fifteen years. Plenty of people have tried to stop me. A cat and a dog won't succeed where they failed!'

'If anything, it would be Eccles the parrot who *sucks seed*,' Mr Dog joked weakly, although to human ears it came out as a growl.

Angus jumped quickly down from the shelf, nimbly avoiding the broken glass. His lead landed with a clatter beside him.

'Mr Bernwood is giving me five thousand pounds for that Scottish wildcat tonight,' Noel announced. 'So catch him, Jan. Catch him and keep hold of him this time!'

Mr Dog stood protectively in front of the kitten. He bared his teeth and let rip with his scariest barks.

'Desi, put a dart in that dog,' snapped Noel. 'NOW!'

But, before Desi could even take aim, there was a sudden commotion overhead. Eccles the parrot burst through the hinged door of her cage and launched into noisy flight – straight at the humans!

'You must have unhooked the door after all, Angus,' yowled Mr Dog. 'Well done!'

Eccles pecked and flapped at Desi and Jan. Desi dropped his gun. Jan took a swipe at the colourful bird.

'Don't hurt that parrot!' Noel roared. 'She's worth a fortune!'

'Exotic pets!' Eccles squawked in Noel's voice. 'Keep it secret!' Then she pecked at Noel's hair. 'Owwww!' Noel fell over backwards. The other animals hooted, hissed and yipped to see their cruel handler get a big-beaked comeuppance!

With Noel down, Eccles returned to her winged attack on Desi and Jan.

'Shall we run for it, Mr Dog?' cried Angus.

'Yes,' said Mr Dog, picking up the other end of Angus's lead. 'Only this time we're going to run straight *at* them!'

Mr Dog stayed slightly behind Angus and they kept apart so that the lead was stretched taut and tight between them. Then both doggy and moggy charged forward together! The lead made a very effective tripwire! Desi and Jan caught their ankles on it and fell over on their faces as the animals raced out through the door.

'We did it!' Angus gasped as they bolted
through another storeroom and out into a fancy
lounge. From there, Mr Dog led Angus through
two more rooms into a grand wooden hallway.
Noel's house was enormous. She had clearly
made a lot of money from selling such special
animals.

'*SQUAWK!*' Eccles came flying overhead.
'That was fun,' she said.

'Thanks for your help,' said Mr Dog. 'But we're
not out of the woods yet.'

'We *are*, Mr Dog,' said Angus, confused. 'We're
in a building.'

'It's just a saying, Angus.' Mr Dog skidded to a

stop on the polished floorboards. 'But yes, we *are* in a building. I just wish I knew how to get out again!'

Ahead of them stood the front door – but it was closed, of course. Mr Dog jumped up and yanked on the handle, but it was too stiff to pull down. Angus tried swinging from it, but it was no good. They had no way to get the door open.

'Two people are coming up the path,' Eccles reported from the window. '*Squawk!*'

A second later, the doorbell rang.

Mr Dog turned to the parrot. 'Ask who's there in Noel's voice!'

'Who is it?' said Eccles in perfect imitation.

'Mr Bernwood is here, Noel,' boomed the familiar voice of Sawyer the hunter from the other side of the door. 'I've escorted him all the way from his car as you requested.'

Mr Bernwood spoke in a softer voice: 'I'm here to collect the wildcat you've acquired for me . . .'

'Where did those beasts go?' Noel bellowed from a couple of rooms away.

Mr Dog looked at the parrot. 'Tell Sawyer to open the door!'

Eccles said in Noel's voice: 'Open the cage.'

'The *cage*?' said Angus. 'It's a door. Even I can see it's a door!'

'I've never heard Noel say "door",' Eccles

squawked. 'I can't copy something if I've never heard it!' She switched back to Noel's voice. 'Open! Very rare. Open.'

'She wants me to let you in,' said Sawyer. 'I suppose she must have her hands full.'

A heavy key turned in the lock and the handle twisted down. But now Desi had made it into the hallway and was pointing his tranquilliser gun. 'Here they are, Noel!' he shouted and he fired!

As the door swung open, Mr Dog dived aside and swept Angus out of the way.

The dart flew on through the open door and struck Sawyer in the ankle! 'OW!' he bellowed.

'You idiot!' He started dancing about on one foot

in pain and knocked Mr Bernwood over into a

bush.

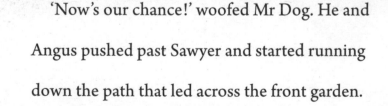

'Now's our chance!' woofed Mr Dog. He and

Angus pushed past Sawyer and started running

down the path that led across the front garden.

On brilliant green wings, Eccles flew ahead of them both. Desi charged after them, just as Mr Bernwood scrambled back up – and accidentally knocked him down again!

'Stop them!' Noel screamed. 'Oh, Mr Bernwood, please forgive me . . .'

'Was that my wildcat?' he cried. 'What is going on around here?'

You have no idea! thought Mr Dog. He raced on through the gardens with Angus beside him. 'Eccles!' he panted. 'You can see from up there. Is the way ahead safe?'

'No!' the parrot squawked. 'Two people are running towards you. Turn back! Turn back!'

'We can't,' said Angus, looking behind. 'Desi the hunter is still after us.'

He huddled close to Mr Dog as the furious Desi charged into sight.

'It seems our escape was all for nothing!' said Mr Dog.

Chapter Ten

TURNING THE TABLES

Mr Dog barked at Desi, but the hunter just smirked and raised his gun.

'This time I won't miss,' he said.

'Wrong!' came a deep roar from the bushes beside him – as an eight-foot grizzly bear burst into sight.

'Zeus!' cheered Mr Dog.

Zeus knocked Desi's arm down with a swipe of his powerful paw. The hunter shot a dart straight into his own foot!

'Way to go, bear!' Angus ran up to Desi, who was already swaying on his feet. 'And as for you, Mr Shooty Man . . .' The kitten jumped up at Desi and pushed him over.

Desi did not get up again.

Zeus got down on all fours and sniffed him. 'Do you think he's got any tuna sandwiches on him?'

'I'd give you a hundred sandwiches if I could!' said Mr Dog. 'Where did you spring from anyway?'

'I ran into Mike and Iona in the forest,' said Zeus. 'I've been helping them get past the hunters guarding this place.'

'Who are Mike and Iona?' Angus asked.

'They have excellent snacks,' Zeus explained.

'They're TV journalists,' Mr Dog said more helpfully. 'They've been trying to get evidence of what Noel is up to . . . and look! Here they are now!'

Mr Dog watched the couple coming cautiously out of the shadows. '*They* are the two people Eccles spotted and warned us about!' He shook his head in disbelief – and, as he did so, a small black cylinder attached to a clip fell out from his handkerchief collar.

Angus nudged it with his little pink nose. 'What's that?' he asked.

'It looks like a little microphone,' said Mr Dog.

'Something humans use to make their voices louder . . . or to sing into . . . or –'

His explanation was cut short by Nasty Noel bursting into sight. 'Stop right there!' She pointed a hunting rifle at Zeus, but kept her eyes on Mike and Iona. 'You two are trespassing on private property. Get out of here.'

'Sorry, Noel,' said Iona. 'I know that no one's ever stopped you trading in wild animals before, but that's all about to change.'

'Right,' said Mike, who had brought out his camera. 'And we were actually invited on to your property just after Mr Bernwood drove through the gates. Your guard was so scared by Zeus he ran away and told us to do whatever we liked . . .'

Noel frowned. 'How do you know about Mr
Bernwood?'

'We've been listening in on your
conversations,' said Iona with a smile. 'Guess
what? I hid a little radio microphone in the hanky
round that dog's neck!'

'Indeed you did!'
woofed Mr Dog
happily. He gave
Iona a doggy
grin, full of
admiration for
her cleverness.

'Every growl and whimper has been recorded,' Iona went on. 'Along with everything you and your hunters said in front of that plucky mutt.' She produced a digital audio recorder and pressed a button. Noel's voice came out of it: '*I've been trapping and trading wild animals for fifteen years . . .*'

Noel's face darkened. 'That's not real proof. It could be someone impersonating my voice.'

Mr Dog woofed up to Eccles. 'Why don't you show Noel what an impersonator sounds like?'

Eccles came flapping down and perched on Zeus's shoulder. 'Exotic pets! Very rare, best price,' she said. 'Keep it secret. *SQUAWK!*'

Iona laughed. 'How could a parrot say those things in your voice if you never said them yourself?'

'Beautiful job, parrot,' Mike told Eccles. 'And I've got it all on video!'

'We've already sent footage of your dancing bear to the police,' Iona added. 'They really don't like dangerous wild animals roaming the countryside.'

'Dangerous?' said Zeus in shock. 'Me?'

'You're only dangerous to sandwiches!' Mr Dog chuckled.

'The police are on their way right now with a vet and an animal-welfare officer,' Mike told

Noel. 'As yours is the only property in this area,

they wanted to search the grounds.'

Iona nodded. 'And, once we've played the

police our recordings, I think they're going to

want to talk to you about lots of other things too.'

Icily, Noel turned and stalked away.

Mike went after her with his camera. 'While

we wait for the police together, do you think Mr

Bernwood would give us an interview?' he called.

'We'd like to know why he's paying you five

thousand pounds to own a protected animal you

trapped illegally . . .'

Iona was about to follow, but then turned

back. Zeus watched her. Eccles, still perched on

the bear's shoulder, cocked her head to one side. Angus looked up at her and mewed a thank-you.

As for Mr Dog, he simply sat on his haunches and raised a paw in thanks. Iona crouched beside him and patted his head.

'You saved the day, dog,' she murmured. 'Not just because you carried that microphone to right where it was needed . . . but because, in some crazy way, I think you've been watching out for all these animals the whole time.'

Mr Dog gave his widest doggy grin and barked proudly.

Iona nodded and smiled. 'Well, the garden gates are shut so I don't think any of you critters can get out again. I'd better catch up with Mike. I've wanted to take Noel down for years – and I don't want to miss the big moment!'

Iona hurried away towards Noel's house, whistling to herself.

Mr Dog turned to Angus, Eccles and Zeus. 'Well, my friends,' he said, 'I rather think it's time you went back to your cages.'

'What?' Angus cried. 'No way!'

'It won't be for long,' Mr Dog assured him. 'You heard Mike and Iona. They now have the evidence they need to close down Noel's business. The police are on their way, with an animal-welfare officer. You'll all be taken to proper homes, to live your best and wildest lives.'

Zeus considered. 'I suppose that's all right then,' he said. The big bear turned and trooped back towards the exercise yard. With a squawk, Eccles flapped after him.

'Do I have to go too, Mr Dog?' the kitten said.

'You do, Angus,' said Mr Dog. 'But don't worry. You'll soon be taken back to the Scottish highlands and set free to enjoy the wild once more.'

Angus sighed happily. 'Do you think I'll see Mama again? My *real* mama, I mean?'

'I'm sure of it,' said Mr Dog with a smile. 'Especially now that I know how remarkable wildcat noses are at sniffing out a scent! And I hope your cheetah-mama will be reunited with her own cubs too!'

With his friends willingly back in their cages, Mr Dog waited out in the grounds. He watched as police cars came up the drive, their blue lights flashing through the darkness. He saw them leave hours later, taking Noel, Sawyer, Desi and Jan to the police station to give statements. And he heard the animal-welfare officer say that the other hunters would be rounded up in no time.

Best of all, Noel's menagerie would be checked over by a vet and kept somewhere safe until they could be taken to new and happier homes.

As the sun began to rise, Mr Dog jumped up
at the window that looked on to the animals'
enclosure. Angus saw him and waved. The
cheetah, sitting beside him, gave him a long look
and simply nodded her thanks.

Mr Dog nodded back. Then he barked again
to Angus, Zeus and Eccles, and turned away.
'My snout is good at sniffing out scents too,'
he murmured. 'The next time I visit the
highlands, I'll keep a nostril open for
Angus and see how he's grown.

Perhaps the wildcat and the wild dog will have some new adventures together some day.'

Mr Dog chuckled. 'After all – it would be a proper dog-and-*cat*-astrophe if we didn't!'

Notes from the Author

All around the world, hundreds of millions of different animals of all kinds of shapes and sizes are kept as exotic pets. Some people just want to sell them and make money. Some people buy them because they genuinely love animals. Some people buy them because they find them exciting. It's amazing how something like a big cat or a bear can look when you see it on television or social media! But if you think a new puppy or kitten is trouble in the house, it's nothing compared to a wildcat or a tiger cub!

I'm lucky that in my travels I have been able to see so many amazing animals in the wild. When you see them out there, in Africa or South America, you realise how different they actually are and that you really can't look

126

after a wild animal like an ordinary pet in an ordinary home. It needs the right food to eat, and it needs its own natural place to live and sleep. It's important to make sure wild animals have a home where they belong. Remember, too, that exotic pets are often shipped thousands of miles to reach their new owners and as many as four out of five animals will die as they travel to their new home or within a year of their captivity. If we care about animals we have to stop the illegal trade in wild animals and I hope that people will continue to join the many brave and brilliant heroes who are already out there fighting to bring it to an end.

Have you read Mr Dog's other adventures?

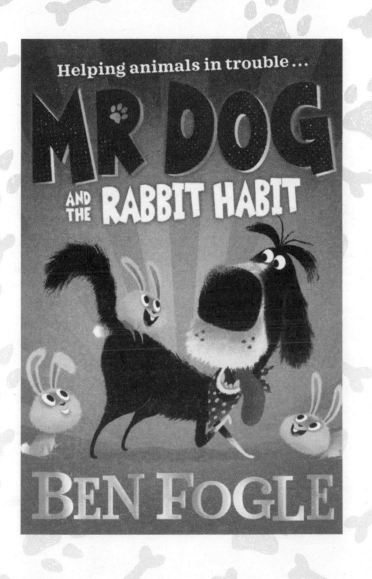

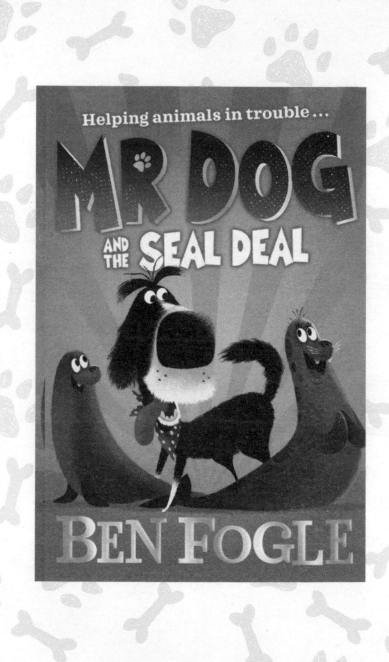

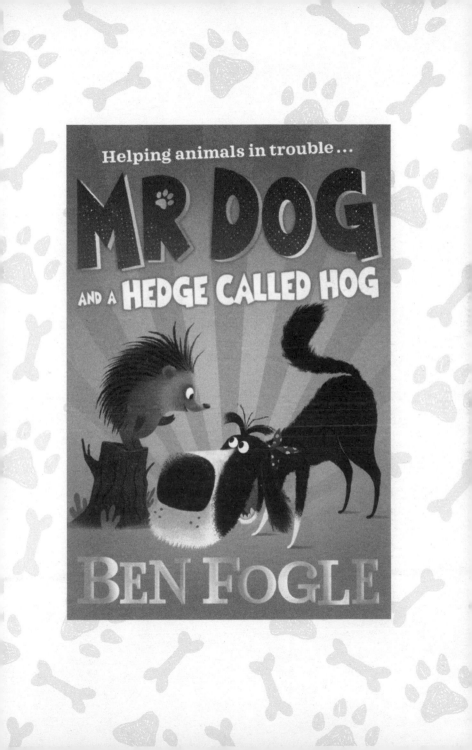

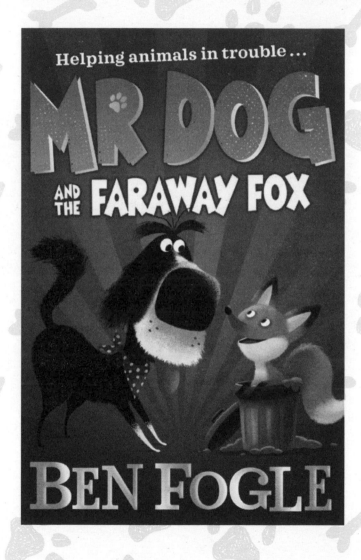

Helping animals in trouble...

MR DOG

AND THE FARAWAY FOX

BEN FOGLE